WHITNEY STOWS AWAY ON NOAH'S ARK

and learns how to deal with peer pressure

THE EMERALD BIBLE COLLECTION

THERESE JOHNSON BORCHARD

ILLUSTRATIONS BY WENDY VANNEST

PAULIST PRESS

NEW YORK / MAHWAH, N.J.

Library of Congress Cataloging-in-Publication Data

Borchard, Therese Johnson.
    Whitney stows away on Noah's ark : and learns how to deal with peer pressure / by Therese Johnson Borchard ; illustrated by Wendy VanNest.
        p. cm. -- (The Emerald Bible collection)
    Summary: When Whitney fails to stand up for a classmate who is being ridiculed, her emerald Bible enables her to go back in time and board the Ark with Noah as he saves the animals from the great flood.
    ISBN 0-8091-6674-7 (alk. paper)
    1. Noah (Biblical figure)--Juvenile fiction. [1. Noah (Biblical figure)--Fiction. 2. Noah's ark--Fiction. 3. Time travel--Fiction. 4. Peer pressure--Fiction.] I. VanNest, Wendy, ill. II. Title. III. Series.

PZ7.B64775 Whk 2000
[Fic]

                                                                    99-055102

Published by Paulist Press
997 Macarthur Boulevard
Mahwah, New Jersey 07430

www.paulistpress.com

Printed and bound in the United States of America

The Emerald Bible Collection
is dedicated
to the loving memory of
Whitney Bickham Johnson

TABLE OF CONTENTS

NANA'S EMERALD BIBLE

It was a warm August morning the day the Bickham family moved from their Michigan home to a residence in a western suburb of Chicago. Mr. Bickham's mother, Nana, who had lived with the family for some time, had passed away in February of that same year. Not long after, Mr. Bickham landed a great new job; however, it meant the whole family would have to leave everything that was familiar to them in Michigan and start again in Chicago.

It was especially hard on Whitney and Howard, the two Bickham children. They had grown accustomed to their school in Michigan and had several friends there. They didn't want to have to start over at a new school. Whitney, especially, was heartbroken about moving away from Michigan, for Nana's death alone had been very difficult on her. For Whitney, the Bickhams' Michigan home was filled with wonderful memories of Nana that she did not want to leave behind.

Nana and Whitney had had a very special friendship. Since Mrs. Bickham worked a day job that kept her very busy, it was Nana that had cared for Whitney from the time she was a baby. Growing up, Whitney spent endless hours with Nana. Her most wonderful memories of Nana centered around those afternoons when the two would go down to the basement and read stories from the Bible. Nana would sit on her favorite chair and read a story to

Whitney that related in some way to a problem Whitney was having. As Whitney sat on her grandma's lap listening to the story, her own situation always became a little clearer.

When Nana became sick and knew she was going to die, she called Whitney into her room and said:

"Dear Whitney, you know how special you are to me. I want you to have something that will always bring you home to me. I have a favorite possession that I'd like to leave with you—my Emerald Bible. Every time you open this special book, you will find yourself in another world—at a place far away from your own, and in a time way before your birth. But I will be right there with you."

Nana was so weak that she could barely go on, but, knowing the importance of her message, she pushed herself to say these last words:

"Whatever you do in the years

ahead, keep this Bible with you, as it will help you with all of life's most difficult lessons. And remember, when you open its pages, I am there with you."

As Nana closed her eyes to enter into an eternal sleep, Whitney spotted the beautiful Emerald Bible that lay at Nana's side. It sparkled like a massive jewel, and on its cover were engraved the words, "Lessons of Life."

And so it began that Whitney would take her Emerald Bible to the basement of the new home and, sitting on Nana's favorite chair, would look up to heaven and ask Nana to help her choose a story to read.

CHAPTER ONE

THE COMPUTER NERD

Six weeks had already passed by since Whitney's first day of class at her new school in Chicago. She had managed to find a group of friends almost as much fun as Molly and Sue back home in Michigan. Chicago definitely had more going on than her quiet suburb in Michigan. Yet she missed the familiarity of her old neighborhood streets.

It seemed as though things moved more quickly in Chicago. For example, the latest movies came to Chicago a couple of weeks before they showed in Michigan. Whitney had called Molly and Sue a couple of times last month to see what they thought of a certain movie, and they had told her that it wasn't out yet.

It was like that with everything: music, videos, computer games. For the most part, Whitney enjoyed living in a place that was at the cutting edge of everything. However, with some things—like technology—it seemed to be getting out of control.

There was this guy in Whitney's class who brought a laptop computer with him to class every day. He'd type notes the whole time the teacher was talking. Whitney would hear things beeping throughout the entire class. And in science class it got even more complex. Instead of loosely sketching on a piece of scrap paper the diagrams that Mr. Peters, the science teacher, would draw on the chalkboard, he'd pull up a spread sheet measured in squares of one-sixteenth of an inch each, so that his diagram would perfectly match the one on the board.

The guy's name was Pat Chan, but everyone mockingly called him "PC" (for "personal computer"). He was Japanese

American and a whiz at everything from computer games to math.

Every day in class, it was the same. Mr. Peters would start drawing the planets of the solar system or something like that, and Pat would pull up an electronic chart on which to draw his model. Then someone would throw out a smart remark, making fun of him.

The other day, Mario, a sharp-witted Italian boy who occasionally filled in for the class clown, remarked aloud in class, "Why bother putting it up on the board, Mr. Peters, PC's got it saved somewhere in that hard drive of his." The day before, Allen Green, captain of the soccer team, threw out another wise comment: "No offense, Teacher, but PC's charts are much more precise. Can we use his for the exam?"

Most of the time it was innocent fun, and Pat's feelings weren't hurt. Even Whitney threw out a comment now and then to her friends within hearing distance. But lately the remarks had seemed mean-spirited, and Pat was no longer laughing at them. Whitney felt sorry for him.

She would never tell anyone this, but she secretly respected him and admired his skills. She was struggling in science class because she didn't take very good notes. When she got home to study, she could never make sense of the drawings she had copied from the board. In a way, she wished she had Pat's computer skills so that she could take better notes.

Mercury Hg
Hydrogen H
Alumin...

However, since she was still pretty new to the school, she didn't want to do anything that made her stand out. There was no way that she was going to defend Pat and tell everyone to lay off.

She was sure that if she did that, she would be ridiculed along with him. And things were going pretty well at school. She did not want to risk it.

So she went along with the fun, pretending that she thought Pat was weird for taking careful notes with his computer.

One day, in particular, the fun turned cruel. Allen yelled out before class began, "Hey, Weirdo Whiz, how about taking notes for all of us and printing them out after class? That is the only way you'll make any friends, you know!"

Mario chimed in, "Maybe the electronic nerd can't do anything but take notes." And turning to Pat, he continued, "PC, can you do anything else besides take notes? What does your mom feed you at night? Batteries?"

Mr. Peters walked into the classroom just in time to catch the end of the last comment.

"Alright, everyone, that's enough! We're coming to the end of the chapter, and I am scheduling a test for next Friday. After the test, when all of you have scored A's, if you want to make fun of Pat, that's up to you. But until then, I suggest you keep your comments to yourselves."

Whitney cringed as Mr. Peters set the date for the test. Science, like math, was not her thing. And she had not been doing the reading assignments, so she had tons of catching up to do. Plus, next Friday was the big soccer game. She was planning on practicing a lot this week.

She felt the knot in her stomach grow tighter and tighter. She looked at her friend Tonya with an expression of fear and disgust.

"Whitney, you don't look so hot," Tonya said, noticing that Whitney's face had turned a pale green. "It will be okay. We just have some studying to do."

"But Tonya, look at these notes!" Whitney replied, lifting the notebook in front of her. It was opened to yesterday's notes, which looked like a mess of spiderwebs.

"Yeah," Tonya responded. "Mine don't look much better."

"What are we going to do?" Whitney said, beginning to panic.

"I don't know. We'll talk about it tonight."

Tonya was always calm. If the school was on fire and she was the only one left in the building, she wouldn't panic. She would keep her cool and look for the safest exit. Whitney wished she could be more like that. The slightest thing would throw her off, such as a sly comment that was meant to poke fun. Tonya, Maria, and Le Ly called her paranoid at times. Whitney knew that she was probably just a little insecure. But she had reason to be, she rationalized. She was trying to fit into a new group of friends at a new school in a new city.

There was no more time to talk about the test. Mr. Peters went on with the day's lesson. Pat did not let all the ridicule stop him from taking good notes. He concentrated on the drawings as normal. At the end of class, he saved all his work and quit the program he was using. And as always, two minutes before class ended, Pat's computer made this strange beeping noise. It was a more reliable signal that class was over than the school bell.

A couple of the guys surrounded Pat as soon as he reached the hallway outside the science classroom.

"Hey, Pat, how about sharing your

notes with some of us for the test?"
Mario asked.

"I don't think so after today's
jokes. They were more mean than
funny. Besides, you can manage. Or at
least I hope so," Pat responded.

Pat quickly walked away from
them and didn't look back. "What nerve
they have to ask me for my notes after
harassing me for weeks," Pat thought to
himself.

As Whitney made her way to her locker, she thought more about the upcoming test. She wished that she could go back in time and stand up for Pat today when everyone was making fun of him. Had she defended him earlier, she wouldn't feel bad asking for his help in studying for the test. He may have even offered to help her. But she didn't dare ask him at this point, having done nothing to help him when he needed it most.

As soon as she reached her locker, she gathered her books to take home and study.

"Yuck!" Whitney said aloud as she stuffed her book bag. "Math and science. This is not going to be a fun week."

Before slamming her locker shut, Whitney found a note someone had slipped through the door of the locker. It read, "Whitney, call me when you get home. Let's combine science notes. Talk to you later, Tonya."

"Little good that will do," the eleven-year-old remarked hopelessly as she walked away.

When Whitney reached home, Bailey ran to the door and showered the fifth-grader with licks. Bailey always lifted Whitney's spirits, no matter how low she was feeling. The furry guy was the next best thing to Nana. His generous licks were a good substitute for the homemade cookies Nana used to have waiting for Whitney and her brother, Howard, when they arrived home from school.

"There is only one thing that is going to make me feel better. Right, Bailey?" Whitney leaned down to pet her favorite pup.

Bailey jumped up to lick her more, as if he were responding to her question. Then he began to bark.

"That's right, Bailey . . . Nana's Emerald Bible," Whitney said to him. She treated him to a snack before story hour began.

"Do you want to join me?" Whitney asked her companion, who barked with enthusiasm.

The twosome walked down the basement stairs and began looking for the Emerald Bible. Whitney always hid it, because she considered it a secret treasure. No one knew about the Bible besides her mom and Bailey. And she liked it that way. It was her special way of connecting with Nana, and she didn't want to share it with anyone else. At least not at this point.

Whitney forgot that she had shoved the Bible underneath the couch after the last story.

"Where in the world did I put Nana's Emerald Bible?" she asked herself just as Bailey began barking.

The pup walked toward her carrying the Emerald Bible in his mouth.

"Bailey, where did you find my Bible?" Whitney asked her furry detective. And Bailey turned his head around and looked at the couch.

"You're so smart! I forgot that I left it under the couch!"

Whitney sat down on Nana's favorite chair and snuggled into its comfy cushions. She looked to Bailey and asked him, "Are you ready for another one of Nana's stories?"

After a nice, wet lick from him, she opened the emerald cover. Rays of light emerged as she thumbed through its delicate pages. Her eyes stopped at a paragraph, and she began to read aloud:

"The Lord saw that the wickedness of humankind was great on the earth, and He was sorry that he had made humankind. He said to himself, 'I will blot out from the earth the human beings I have created—people together with animals and creeping things and birds of the air, for I am sorry that I have made them.' But there was one old man the Lord wanted to spare, and his name was Noah."

CHAPTER TWO

NOAH'S BIG BOAT

As soon as Whitney looked up from reading the paragraph, she found herself once again in a world long before her time. She was standing in front of a massive boat. It was humongous in size—by far the biggest boat she had ever seen. It was even larger than the cruise ships she often saw advertised on TV.

There was something very strange about the boat. For one thing, it was sitting on the rocky ground in the middle of a vast, arid land. Whitney looked around for water, but she could not find anything. And Bailey hadn't gone off running in any direction, which

he always did when water was nearby. He could usually smell a lake or ocean if Whitney and he were within a mile's distance from it.

A group of men were busy at work on the boat. It was nearly finished, with only some last-minute construction to do, namely, the door of the ark, which was to go on the side. Like a skyscraper, the huge boat was an optical illusion. That is, it seemed to be closer than it really was.

Whitney held Bailey by his collar as she walked toward the boat to get a better look. It was the length of a modern oil tanker, the height of a three- to four-story house, and the width of a couple of classrooms put together.

She heard the young men working on the boat call the name "Noah." She guessed that it was Noah's boat and that he was the older man directing everyone.

"Uh, excuse me, sir," Whitney politely asked the man beside her. He was dressed in a robe similar to the ones worn by the men in the other Bible stories. "What is the boat for?"

"Isn't that the question of the year? Why, everyone wants to know why

Noah is building a boat in this drought. I can't even remember the last time it rained. All of our crops are dead. And . . ."

Whitney rudely interrupted the man.

"Wait a minute. You mean there is no water nearby?" she asked. The young girl was dumbfounded that there was no lake or ocean, no body of water big enough for the boat, yet everyone was scurrying about to finish the thing.

"But . . . ," Whitney continued with her questions, expecting the man to whom she was speaking to interrupt her with the logical explanation. But he let her finish.

"But, I don't understand," she said, finally able to complete her sentence.

"Well, join the club, because none of us do either. Noah's gone out of his mind, and his family is even nuttier than he is for going along with his plan. If I were his son, I'd talk some sense into the old man.

"A flood . . . ," the man continued, "in the middle of the desert. Yeah, right! What is he thinking?"

"A flood?" Whitney asked. Now she was really confused. "Noah thinks there will be a flood?"

"Oh yeah, haven't you heard? This nut says that God told him that there was going to be a flood and to build a boat big enough to carry two of each kind of animal." The man, who had been staring at the boat since the beginning of their conversation, finally looked at Whitney. He was baffled by her clothes and her strange accent.

"Where the heck have you been, anyway? It's been the talk of the town for the last year or more."

"Uhh, well . . . ," Whitney quickly

replied, "I don't live here. I am just passing through."

"Ahh. I see," the man nodded his head, still staring at her with a weird expression on his face.

"Yep, Noah and his family believe that God is going to flood the earth and that they will be the only people to survive. He thinks that they are the 'chosen ones.'

"I don't buy that for one second." The man continued talking about the situation for at least a half hour. Whitney had heard the whole story . . . about how God had come to Noah disappointed with the wickedness that was going on and had decided to destroy the earth in a flood. But God liked Noah and found him to be a good man. So God instructed his chosen one to build a boat and, when he was done, to gather on it two of every living creature—one male and one female. According to Noah, God even gave him the dimensions of the boat and explained how he should build it.

CHAPTER THREE

RAIN, RAIN, GO AWAY!

Whitney looked at the crowd that had gathered around the boat. Most of the people talked among themselves in small circles. They were laughing as they pointed at the big boat.

Bailey suddenly ran off to explore the boat, and Whitney went after him, running in between the circles of conversation. She could overhear the talk among the people.

"What a crazy man he is!" one of the women said to her husband. "I knew Noah was a bit strange . . . but not to this extent!"

Another man yelled to one of

Noah's sons. "Hey Shem, when was the last time we had rain? Can you remember that far back?"

The man said it loud enough for those around him to hear. There were lots of chuckles coming from every direction. The townspeople seemed to be having the time of their lives at Noah's expense. The boatbuilder and his family were the butt of all the jokes with no exception. And the remarks were growing sharper and meaner with each passing moment. No matter where the ten-year-old and her pup walked, she could hear unkind remarks about Noah, his wife, his sons, and their wives.

Whitney bent down to tighten Bailey's leash. She was beginning to feel uncomfortable.

"What if what Noah says is true?" she whispered to Bailey. "What if God is really planning on flooding the world?"

The fifth-grader had a reason to

worry. The situation of Noah and the flood reminded her a little of her own situation with Pat Chan in science class. It was all fun and games there, too, until Mr. Peters had announced the upcoming test. Then Whitney and everyone else began to envy Pat for having prepared for the exam.

The outcome at school was still to be determined, but Whitney was sure it was grim. At best she would get by with a D in science, which would upset her mom and dad. That meant that she would have to spend more time on her schoolwork and less time on soccer and other sports.

Whitney was glad to see that Noah and his family weren't too affected by all the mockery. They concentrated on their work and blocked out the laughter and remarks of the community.

Noah's wife was busy gathering seed and other food for the trip. Shem, Ham, and Japheth—Noah's three sons—

worked on finishing the door of the ark. And their wives (Noah's daughters-in-law) had started to gather two of every kind of creature to take into the ark.

Everyone except for Noah and his family were mere spectators. No one offered to help with anything. They were busy watching for something to go wrong so that they could poke fun. The latest jokes were on Shem, for falling with a heavy load of wood during a trip to the door of the ark, and on Noah's wife, for running frantically after the two bears that had darted off with her food.

"Hey, Noah," one of the men shouted from the crowd. "I think I hear thunder!" He was being sarcastic, and everyone roared with laughter.

But only seconds later the loudest rumble of thunder that Whitney had ever heard in her life echoed through the place. It was so intense that the ground beneath her and Bailey began to tremble.

And there was silence for the first time in a long while among the crowd. Everyone looked at one another in disbelief, for there had been no rainstorms in months.

Everyone, including Noah and his family, looked up to see that the sky had become an ominous gray. Following a strong gust of wind, the heavens broke open and rain began to fall: mist and sprinkles first, and then a heavy downpour and hail.

"OK, guys. Listen to me. It's time to start boarding the ark," Noah said to his family. "Gather the last of the seed and begin to organize the animals into like pairs."

Noah directed his family like a skilled orchestra director pointing at each musician when it was time to play. He was certainly enjoying this moment. He had earned it. Not only was he a good and righteous man, but Noah was also obedient to God, even in the face of ridicule and mockery. Anyone else would have laughed at God's instructions and gone on with his daily chores. The boatbuilder had tremendous faith in God, and his work showed it.

Noah's entire family enjoyed the

silence of the people. No one could say another word until the rain stopped. And it didn't.

When the water level had reached Whitney's ankles, she and Bailey, with the rest of the crowd, began to worry. People scrambled in every direction, making their way home to salvage whatever they could. Many had food on the floors of their tents that had spoiled in the rain. The men sought tree branches and began to build ladders and elevated shelters to keep themselves and their families dry. However, as it continued to rain the ground became slippery and nothing seemed to hold.

Whitney and Bailey didn't know where to go. They had no home, no tent to run to. Whitney didn't like anyone she had met, nor had she received any invitations. So she and her pup ran to take cover underneath a cypress tree—one that stood tall among the others that had been cut down for wood for the ark.

She observed the amazing procession of creatures streaming into the ark. The wives of Noah's sons had lined up the pairs of insects, birds, and other animals from smallest to largest. First, pairs of ants, spiders, bees, flies, and all kinds of creepy things were taken inside the ark. This was the hardest part for Whitney to

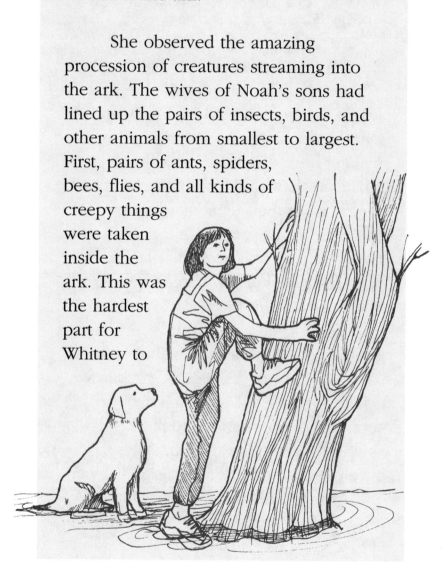

44

watch. She was more afraid of
bugs than bears; a spider
crawling up her leg frightened her
far more than a hungry
tiger chasing after its prey.
She had no desire to board
the ark after she saw the
nest of insects taken
inside.

However, the
spectacle got better as the birds and
small animals boarded the ark. Whitney
loved the zoo, and this was even better.
Before her eyes was every single kind
of feathered vertebrate—wild and
domestic. It had been a long time since
she had seen the colorful feathers of a
peacock or heard the funny sounds of a
parrot. She was tempted to go up closer
and talk to the animals, but she knew
better. She didn't want Noah or any
member of his family to see her. By
now the flood had reached her lower
calves, and she knew that she and

Bailey had to come up with a quick plan. By the time the horses and cattle had made their way inside the ark, the water had reached Whitney's knees, and Bailey was already swimming. Whitney rolled up the pant legs of her denim jumper and squatted down to pick up Bailey. He was noticeably scared.

"It will be OK, Bailey," she whispered to him. "We will find a way to get inside Noah's boat, even if it means having to room with those gross insects for a few days."

The smart fifth-grader looked at the line of animals behind the horses and cattle.

"Bailey, we could hide underneath one of the larger animals. There is plenty of space to hang below their stomachs. What about underneath the giraffe, or the zebra? No, better yet, underneath the elephant. Yeah, the elephant is huge. That would work."

Whitney talked aloud as she finalized her plan. The tricky part was getting from where she was to the elephants without being seen by Noah or anyone in his family.

"OK, Bailey," she instructed her pup, who was now shaking from the cold water. "We are going to sneak behind the line of animals as soon as Noah leads the

giraffes inside the ark. We only have a split second before he comes out again to take care of the zebras, so we have to be quick."

Whitney looked like a spy. She waited behind the cypress tree for her cue. As soon as Noah turned his back and the others were busy with the animals, she darted as quickly as possible in a squat position toward the line of animals. Holding Bailey tightly to herself, she crawled underneath the larger of the elephants.

As gracefully as possible, she secured one of her legs around the hind leg of the elephant and one of her arms around the foreleg of the animal. Then, as if she were climbing the bars of a jungle gym with great skill, she wrapped her other leg around the same hind leg while securing Bailey on her stomach. As soon as she was able to free her other arm, she grabbed the elephant's foreleg and adjusted herself so that there

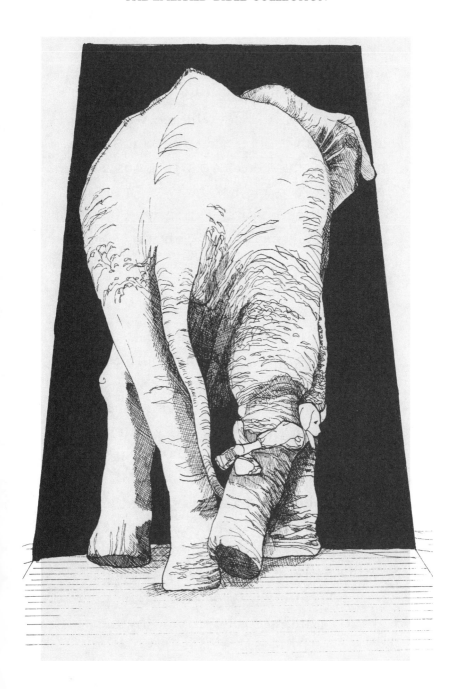

was little room between herself and the elephant's stomach. It was a pretty advanced move, and Whitney was only able to pull it off because her mother had made her take a year of gymnastics when she was eight.

As uncomfortable as it was, she and Bailey hung underneath the belly of the elephant long enough to get inside the door of the ark.

"Where do you want the elephants, Father?" one of Noah's sons asked.

"Take them to the back of the first deck, where the zebras and giraffes are," Noah responded, still enjoying his role as director.

Whitney could barely hold the position until the pair of elephants reached the far end of the lower deck. She released her legs as soon as she heard Noah's son walk away. Bailey had already jumped to the ground by the time her legs hit the floor.

"Whew! We made it, Bailey!" Whitney said to her favorite animal on the ark. "You better stay right here so they don't take you to the upper deck, where the other dogs are. Stick close to me, you hear?"

The two enjoyed a quick stretch before the young man came back with a pair of hippos. The place was filling up, and it didn't smell great. But Whitney was grateful that she and Bailey had made it inside God's only shelter from the flood.

CHAPTER FOUR

ABOARD THE ARK

As the last of the animals boarded the ark, the downpour continued and water began to cover every patch of ground, including the small hills.

Whitney and Bailey could hear the doors of the ark slam shut. Then came a screechy sound of wooden boards rubbing against each other. Whitney guessed the noise meant that Noah was locking the doors securely so that nothing could

escape. For a moment, she felt as though she were a prisoner inside a jail cell—the jail keeper had just locked her in and walked away with the key.

"I guess we'll be here for a while," Whitney said to Bailey, as she assumed a more comfortable sitting position underneath the elephant. Bailey began to whimper. And there was little Whitney could say to comfort him.

Days went by as the rain continued to fall from the heavens. The humongous boat loosened its hold on the ground and began to float aimlessly in the water. Whitney was getting hungry and restless, and Bailey looked weak, so she decided it was time to roam about the boat.

One night at about two A.M. she sneaked into the eating area, where Noah and his family had all of their meals. She found some dried-up fruit and seeds, which she quickly stuffed into her pocket. On the way back to her quarters she stopped by a small window.

As she peered outside for the first time in what seemed like eternity, she realized that nothing but a few fish (and everything on Noah's boat) had probably survived the flood. She saw nothing but water for miles and miles in the distance. No hills. No mountains.

Only a few waves ruffling in the wind.

She thought about how wise and trusting Noah was. She was sure that if she were in his position, she wouldn't have listened to God, especially if it meant being made fun of by everyone except for a few family members. She respected Noah for doing what he knew he had to do to survive, even if it meant suffering through endless jokes and nasty comments.

Whitney thought more about Pat Chan in science class. Like Noah, he had been the topic of every joke and mean remark for a couple of weeks. Although taking notes on a computer wasn't as radical as building a huge boat in the middle of the desert, it certainly made PC stand out in class, whether he liked it or not.

With its beeps and whistles, the computer drew attention to Pat. People did not like that he was doing things a little differently than usual. In some ways it was threatening, especially to those who didn't have Pat's computer skills.

However, like Noah, Pat would probably be the only one to pass the science exam. He would get to enjoy a moment similar to the one Noah just enjoyed—when the rain began to fall and the people grew quiet.

Whitney returned to her place on the ark without getting caught. She began snacking on the treats she had taken from the kitchen and shared some of them with Bailey, who was as famished as she was. Unfortunately she had no way of getting water. She would have to drink from the same dish as the elephants, hippos, giraffes, and zebras.

"Yuck!" Whitney remarked, after swallowing a large mouthful of water from the massive container set out for the large animals. Then she remembered how lucky she was to be aboard the ark. "I guess I can't complain," she muttered to herself underneath her breath. She had to constantly remind herself to be grateful, because the odor inside the boat was getting nastier with each passing day.

CHAPTER FIVE

JAPHETH'S SECRET

Whitney adjusted to her new home with time. She liked petting the animals and talking to them when no one was around. As soon as she heard the sound of human footsteps, she and Bailey would resume their positions underneath the large elephant. And this was working just fine until the day that she sneezed.

Noah's son Japheth was refilling the food and water supply for the zebras, giraffes, and elephants when he heard a sneeze from one of the elephants.

"That didn't sound like an elephant sneeze," he said to both elephants, turning around to look at them.

Whitney held her breath, trying her best not to sneeze again. But the dust from the animal feed tickled her nose.

"Ah choo!" Her second sneeze was louder than the first.

"OK, I know that wasn't from one of you big animals," Japheth said. He was on to something. He guessed correctly that someone was hiding underneath or behind the animals.

"Come out, wherever you are. I know you are hiding in here," Noah's son continued.

Whitney may have gotten

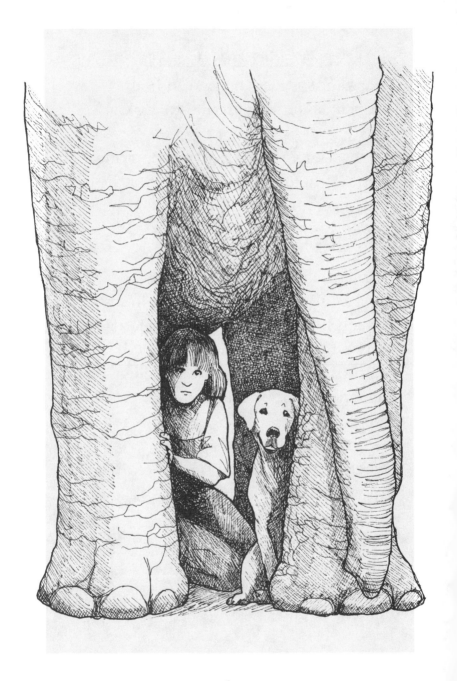

away with her sneezing if Bailey hadn't barked seconds later.

By that point Japheth knew where the strange sounds were coming from. He bent down to peek underneath the larger of the elephants. To his surprise, he found a young girl dressed in strange clothes, and a small, furry dog huddled close to her.

Whitney was trembling with fear.

"Please don't tell Noah!" she begged Japheth. "My dog and I were just passing through your town when it began to rain. We didn't know where to go."

Whitney continued. "But I never uttered an unkind remark about Noah or his family. I respect all of you more than you know."

Japheth could tell by the expression on the young girl's face that she was sincere. He believed her.

"Alright then, I won't tell my father. But you need to stay hidden until we reach land." Japheth was a compassionate man. Yet he was very confused. He had never seen the likes of this girl before. However, before he could ask any questions, he was interrupted.

"Japheth, who are you talking to, dear?" Japheth's wife was feeding the horses and cattle nearby and could hear her husband speaking to someone.

"Just talking to the elephants," Japheth quickly responded.

"Getting a little too lonely are you, sweetheart?" the woman remarked, having a little fun with her husband. She would never believe him if he told her he had found a stowaway and her pup on the boat.

"Listen, before I go," Japheth whispered, "do you need any food or drink?"

"Oh yes," Whitney immediately replied. "I have been drinking from the animals' supply of water. Could you bring me some of my own? And more fruit, seed, and grain?

"Oh, thank you! Thank you very much!" Whitney was ever so grateful.

Japheth kept the secret to himself. Every day thereafter, he visited Whitney and Bailey and made sure that they had enough food and water.

Whitney trusted Japheth, and Japheth admired Whitney. She was different, and he liked that. The two became friends, although they kept their conversations brief in fear of someone overhearing.

Every once in a while Japheth would update Whitney on the flood. For example, one day he gave her news that Noah had opened a window in the ark and released a raven. The bird flew around in every direction and returned to the ark, for the water still covered the earth. A few days later Noah sent out a dove, which also returned to the ark.

One day Japheth came to Whitney and Bailey with exciting news: Noah had released another dove, which had returned with the leaf of an olive tree in its beak. This was a good sign that the waters were beginning to recede.

A week later Noah sent out the dove once more. This time the dove did not return, which meant the bird had found dry land. It would only be a few more days until the large boat itself landed. And everyone was growing impatient.

Japheth promised Whitney that he would ask his father to release the elephants first among the animals. That way he could guard the door during her escape. She was feeling weak and didn't have the strength to pull off the difficult gymnastic move that had enabled her and Bailey to get inside the ark.

Whitney didn't feel the boat hit land, but she knew that must have happened as soon as she saw the huge smile on Japheth's face.

"Good news, Whitney! We've hit land!" Japheth could not hold his excitement inside.

"And my father has agreed to let

the elephants go first. It will be an easy escape."

Japheth expected Whitney to be as excited as he was. But something was definitely bothering her. He didn't have to ask her what was the matter before she started to explain.

"Japheth," she explained. "I left something of great value back where you and your brothers were working on the boat before it started to rain. It was a special book that my grandmother gave me . . . and . . ." The ten-year-old stopped herself before she started to cry. She hated to get emotional in front of people.

Yet few things upset her like this. She was so disappointed in herself for losing her precious Emerald Bible.

"No. You didn't lose it." Whitney looked up at Japheth with confusion and anticipation.

"What do you mean, I didn't lose it?" she asked him.

"Well . . . after we
loaded up the boat, I
did a final check for
valuable items left
behind. I spotted
something green over by
the cypress tree.
We had been cutting
down trees over there,
so I suspected
someone in our
group had
accidentally left it behind
and would eventually claim it.

"You are a lucky girl," he
continued. "Not only did you manage
to board the boat, but your belongings
were taken on, too! You must have
found favor with the Lord, because
things are sure working out right for
you.

"Stay right here, and I'll go get
the green thing you are talking about."
Japheth didn't know what a book was,

or a Bible, but he knew that the square green thing must belong to Whitney.

"Oh Bailey! We will be able to get home, now that we have Nana's Emerald Bible! God has been good to us." Whitney was a believer in miracles after this trip.

As soon as Japheth returned with Whitney's Emerald Bible, she and Bailey prepared to leave the boat. The young girl petted the animals around her for the last time and said a quick good-bye.

She turned to Japheth and thanked him for everything he had done for her.

"Whitney," he said before leading the elephants to the door of the ark, "I believe this was the Lord's plan. Thank him, not me." And so Whitney said a quick prayer of thanksgiving to God.

As soon as Noah's son was sure no one was around, he guided the elephants toward the exit. Whitney squatted down once more underneath the larger of the two, holding Bailey close to her with one arm and holding the Emerald Bible with the other. The girl and her dog stayed between the animal's four legs until they had cleared the door of the ark.

As soon as they were out of sight from the boat, the two darted off like wild animals. Their legs had become stiff from sitting still for so long. So they ran up and down the hills of Ararat, a mountainous area in present-day Turkey. Whitney learned later that the ark had landed on Mount Ararat, the highest mountain in this region.

After a few hours of exercise, she and Bailey rested on the side of a hill. Whitney opened her Emerald Bible to the last page of the story of Noah's ark. She read the last paragraph aloud.

"Noah's ark came to rest on the mountains of Ararat. God then said to Noah, 'Take everything with you from the ark: your wife, your sons, and their wives, and all the creatures you have brought with you, so that everything and everyone may be fruitful and multiply on the earth. I will make a promise with you never to destroy the earth again by flood. And as a sign of this promise, I will make a rainbow in the sky when there is rain. Whenever you see the rainbow, you shall remember my promise to you and to every living creature on earth.'"

CHAPTER SIX

PASS OR FAIL

When Whitney looked up from reading her Emerald Bible, she was happy to find herself once again in Chicago. Nana's chair felt more comfortable than ever. And the basement seemed like heaven compared to her living quarters on Noah's boat.

However, Whitney's peaceful moment was short-lived. Before long, she remembered the haunting science test, for which she had no notes, and the knot in her stomach returned.

"Uh oh," she said to Bailey, who was as content as she was to be home, "the science test. Ugggh. I guess I better give Tonya a call."

But something else was bothering the fifth-grader aside from the science test. She felt bad about not sticking up for Pat in class. Spending so much time with Noah and his family made her realize that it was no fun being the subject of mockery. People had been unkind to Pat, much like they had been to Noah and his family. And she was not innocent. She did not do anything to defend PC. She did not help him. And occasionally, she told a few jokes herself.

Whitney knew she owed Pat an apology. In a strange way, she felt like she owed it to her friend Japheth as well. Even though he didn't know anything about the Pat situation, Noah's son trusted her and admired her. She knew that Japheth would be disappointed in her if she didn't do anything to support someone who was rejected by the people, much like he had been. Even if Pat never wanted to

72

talk to Whitney again, at least she would have done her part to correct her wrongdoing.

The ten-year-old decided to call Pat before calling Tonya. She remembered her Nana's advice: Always do the harder things first, and get them out of the way. And whenever she thought of her late grandmother, she got the strength to do whatever she needed to do.

Whitney looked up Pat's number in the school directory and said a quick prayer to Nana before dialing the number. To her surprise, Pat answered the phone.

"Hello?"

"Ahh, hi Pat, it's Whitney from science class."

"I bet you want to know if I will share my notes with you, right?" Pat asked. Obviously people had been calling him up all afternoon begging for his help.

"Umm. No. Actually, I was calling to apologize for not doing anything to help you earlier this week."

"Oh." Pat was taken aback. No one had expressed any kind of regret for the jokes.

"Well, I just needed to tell you that I am sorry, and that I really respect you for taking such good notes.

"I was also wondering if sometime after the test, you wouldn't mind coaching me on how to take better notes. I could use a lesson or two."

"Ahh, sure," Pat responded. He was really happy that someone respected his notetaking and his computer skills. This pleased him even more than her apology seconds before.

"And, don't worry about not sticking up for me. I know how tough it can be when you are new at school."

Pat was not only smart in science and math. He was insightful about lots of things. He was correct in his thinking about Whitney. It was because she was new at school that she didn't want to do anything that made her stand out.

"Yeah, that's exactly right," Whitney replied, relieved that Pat could understand why she was afraid to help him.

"Listen," Pat continued. "I know you didn't call to get my help. But since you've been so nice, I don't see why I can't share my notes with you."

"You mean it? Really?" Whitney felt as if she had just been invited to board the only boat to survive the flood . . . or the science test.

"Oh, wow. That would be great, Pat. I really appreciate it." Whitney was so excited she could hardly breathe.

"Let's get a study group together. You can invite your friend Tonya, too, if you want. I know you guys are pretty tight."

"Fantastic! Thanks so much, Pat. You have really saved me. You should see what my notes look like. They are a mess."

"You're welcome. But you need to learn how to take better notes. I will teach you sometime after the test."

"I would like that," Whitney told him. She meant it. Pat was a whiz when it came to notetaking, and Whitney could learn from him. This made Pat happy, too, because for once someone looked up to him and valued his skills.

"Call me back after you talk to Tonya."

"I sure will. Talk to you later."

Whitney hung up the phone in

disbelief. She had called up Pat merely to apologize. But now she had a chance of passing the science test. And this meant that she could play in the big soccer game this weekend.

Most importantly, Whitney felt like she had returned a favor to Japheth and Noah's family by sticking up for someone who did things a little differently.

THE EMERALD BIBLE COLLECTION

Also in
THE EMERALD BIBLE COLLECTION

WHITNEY RIDES THE WHALE
WITH JONAH
and learns she can't run away

WHITNEY SEWS JOSEPH'S
MANY-COLORED COAT
and learns a lesson about jealousy

WHITNEY COACHES DAVID
ON FIGHTING GOLIATH
and learns to stand up for herself

WHITNEY SOLVES A DILEMMA
WITH SOLOMON
and learns the importance of honesty

ABOUT THE AUTHOR

Therese Johnson Borchard has always been inspired by the wisdom of the Bible's stories. As a young child, especially, she was intrigued by biblical characters and awed by their courage. She pursued her interest in religion and obtained a B.A. in religious studies from Saint Mary's College, Notre Dame, and an M.A. in theology from the University of Notre Dame. She has published various books and pamphlets in which she creatively retells the great stories of the Judeo-Christian tradition.

ABOUT THE ILLUSTRATOR

Wendy VanNest began drawing as a small, fidgety child seated beside her father at church. He gave her his bulletin to scribble on to help her keep still during the service. People around them began donating their bulletins, asking her for artwork, and at the end of the service, an usher would always give her his carnation boutonniere. As a result of this early encouragement, she pursued her interest and passion in art, and has been drawing ever since.